First published in
Great Britain 2014 by
Egmont UK Limited
This edition published 2019 by Dean,
an imprint of Egmont UK Limited,
The Yellow Building,
1 Nicholas Road, London W11 4AN
www.egmont.co.uk

Text copyright © Adam and Charlotte Guillain 2014
Illustrations copyright © Lee Wildish 2014

The moral rights of the authors and illustrator
have been asserted.
ISBN 978 0 6035 7771 0
70754/001
Printed in Malaysia

Stay safe online. Any website
addresses listed in this book are
correct at the time of going to print.
However, Egmont is not responsible for
content hosted by third parties.
Egmont takes its responsibility to the planet
and its inhabitants very seriously.
We aim to use papers from
well-managed forests run by
responsible suppliers.

For our sweet daughter, Anna

A&C Guillain

Ivy, welcome to the world

L Wildish

MARSHMALLOWS FOR MARTIANS

Adam & Charlotte Guillain

Lee Wildish

DEAN

A boy called George had a marvellous idea
One night as he gazed at the stars,
"I'll go and find out what sweets Martians like best."
So he planned his first mission to Mars.

So George built a rocket and packed up his bag
With a star map and plenty of treats.
The bag full to bursting, he threw out his lunch
So he'd have enough room for his sweets.

He packed lollipops, toffees and chocolate drops.

He took chews with a sharp lemon zest.

There were gobstoppers, jelly beans, humbugs and mints,

And marshmallows - his absolute best!

As George blasted off and zoomed up into space

He looked at his map of the stars.

He checked out the window and steered to the left

And set his course straight towards Mars.

Past satellites, comets and drifting space junk,
George steered without even a bump.

Then he finally saw the red planet appear

And landed on Mars with a . . .

THUMP!

George opened the door in a cloud of red dust.

He jumped out and looked all around.

At first he saw no signs of alien life

But he could hear a very loud sound.

George followed the noise to the top of a rock

And peered down on . . .

...an alien parade!

Their outfits were shocking, but far worse than that
Were the yodelling yowls that they made.

"Excuse me," said George as he jumped from the rock.

"Are you Martians?" he asked with a smile.

"We're Yodlers from Yodel," their leader replied,

"And we've not had a snack for a while."

So George gave the Yodlers some treats that he'd brought.

They gave all the lollies a lick.

Then they gobbled the jelly beans up in a flash

Until they began to feel sick.

"What have you done to our tummies?" they roared.

"I'm terribly sorry," George said,

"But maybe you won't be so greedy next time."

Then he picked up his sweets and he fled.

George hid in a crater but soon heard a BANG

Like the clashing of very loud drums.

He peeped out and spotted an alien band

With cymbals attached to their bums.

"Are you Martians?" called George, running up with a grin.

"No - we're Bangbots from Waabangatoo.
We've come to this planet to bang on our drums,
But we might take a break and eat you!"

"You don't want to eat me,"
said George with a gulp,
"These sweets are much
tastier, you'll see."

The Bangbots crammed gobstoppers into their mouths
And chewed on the toffee with glee.

But the Bangbots soon found that their teeth were stuck tight,
And they howled and they roared in dismay.
Then they started to bang on their cymbals in rage
As George turned and scrambled away.

His sweets almost gone, George slumped to the ground.

"I give up, the Martians have gone.

There are too many visitors making a noise!"

But just then George heard a sweet song . . .

And suddenly little green aliens popped up

With short stumpy legs and three eyes.

They stomped towards George looking grumpy and glum

And they moaned and they wailed with great sighs.

"Are you Martians?" gasped George.

"Yes we are," they replied, "and we're fed up with alien musicians.
They come to our planet and make such a din,
And they never ask us for permission."

"Can you help us?" the Martians begged George in despair
As a rock band from Saturn drew near,
But just as the sound of guitars filled the air
George had a brilliant idea . . .

He picked up the bag with the last of his sweets
And called to the Martians, "Come here!"
Then he took the marshmallows and carefully pushed
One soft sweet into each Martian ear.

"Hooray!" cried the Martians, "We can't hear a thing.
You've made it so peaceful. Yippee!"

Then George jumped in his rocket and waved them goodbye
As he zoomed back to Earth for his tea.